The Knights of the Round Table

Enid Blyton

THE

KNIGHTS
OF THE
ROUND
TABLE

Enid Blyton

Illustrated by Gabrielle Morton

ELEMENT
CHILDREN'S BOOKS

SHAFTESBURY, DORSET · BOSTON, MASSACHUSETTS · MELBOURNE, VICTORIA

Enid Blyton™

Text © Enid Blyton Limited 1930

All Rights Reserved.

Enid Blyton's signature is a trademark of Enid Blyton Limited

For further information please contact www.blyton.com

First published in Great Britain by George Newnes in 1930
First published by Element Children's Books in 1998,
Shaftesbury, Dorset SP7 8BP
Published in the USA in 1998 by Element Books Inc.
North Washington Street, Boston MA 02114

Published in Australia in 1998 by
Element Books Limited and distributed by
Penguin Books Australia Ltd,
487 Maroondah Highway, Ringwood, Victoria 3134

British Library Cataloguing in Publication data available.

Library of Congress Cataloging in Publication data available.

ISBN 1 901881 72 5

Cover design by Gabrielle Morton
Cover illustration © Julie Monks 1998

Inside illustrations © Gabrielle Morton 1998

Typeset by Dorchester Typesetting Group Ltd
Printed and bound in Great Britain by Creative Print and Design

Contents

THE ENCHANTED SWORD   1

THE ROUND TABLE   8

THE FINDING OF THE SWORD EXCALIBUR   12

BALIN, THE KNIGHT OF THE TWO SWORDS   18

PRINCE GERAINT AND THE SPARROWHAWK   27

THE FURTHER ADVENTURES OF GERAINT AND ENID   36

GARETH, THE KNIGHT OF THE KITCHEN   49

SIR GARETH GOES ADVENTURING   56

THE BOLD SIR PEREDUR   68

THE QUEST OF THE HOLY GRAIL   76

THE ADVENTURES OF SIR GALAHAD   81

SIR MORDRED'S PLOT   92

SIR GAWAINE MEETS SIR LANCELOT   99

THE PASSING OF ARTHUR   106

The Enchanted Sword

There once lived a king called Uther Pendragon, who loved the fair Igraine of Cornwall. She did not return his love, and Uther fell ill with grief.

As he lay on his bed, Merlin the Magician appeared before him.

"I know what sorrow is in your heart," he said to the king. "If you will promise what I ask, I will, by my magic art, give you Igraine for your wife."

"I will grant you all you ask," said Uther. "What do you wish?"

"As soon as you and Igraine have a baby son, will you give him to me?" asked Merlin. "Nothing but good shall come to the child, I promise you."

"So be it," said the King. "Give me Igraine for my wife, and you shall have my first son."

It came to pass as Merlin promised. The fair Igraine became Uther Pendragon's wife, and made him very happy. One night a baby son was born to her and the king and Uther looked upon the child's face, and was grieved when he remembered his promise to Merlin.

He named the tiny boy Arthur, and then commanded that he should be taken down to the postern gate, wrapped in a cloth of gold.

"At the gate you will see an old man. Give the child to him," said the king to two of his knights. The knights did as they were commanded, and delivered the baby to Merlin, who was waiting at the postern gate.

The magician took the child to a good knight called Sir Ector, and the knight's wife welcomed the baby, and tended him lovingly, bringing him up as if he were her own dear son.

Not very long after this King Uther fell ill and died. Then many mighty lords wished to be king, and fought one another, so that the kingdom was divided against itself, and could not stand against any foe.

There came a day when Merlin the Magician rode to the Archbishop of Canterbury, and bade him command all the great lords of the land to come to London by Christmas, and worship in the church there.

"There shall you know who is to be king of this country," said Merlin, "for a great marvel shall be shown you."

So the Archbishop sent for all the lords and knights, commanding them to come to the church in London by Christmas, and they obeyed.

When the people came out of church, a cry of wonder was heard – for there, in the churchyard, was a great stone, and in the middle of it was an anvil of steel a foot high. In the anvil was thrust a beautiful sword, and around it, written in letters of gold upon the stone, were these words:

Who so pulleth out this sword from this stone and anvil is rightwise king born of all England.

Lords and knights pressed round the sword and marveled to see it thrust into the stone, for neither sword nor stone had been there when they went into the church.

Then many men caught hold of the sword and tried to pull it forth, but could not. Try as they would, they could not move it an inch. It was held fast, and not even the strongest knight there could draw it forth.

"The man is not here that shall be king of this realm," said the archbishop. "Set ten men to guard the stone day and night. Then, when New Year's Day is come, we will hold a tournament, and the bravest and strongest in the kingdom shall joust one with another. Mayhap by that time there shall come the one who will draw forth the sword, and be hailed as king of this fair land."

Now, when New Year's Day came, many Lords and knights rode on the field to take part in the tournament. With them went the good knight Sir Ector, to whom Merlin had given the baby Arthur some years before.

Sir Ector had brought up the boy with his own son, Sir Kay, and had taught him all the arts of knighthood, so that he grew up brave and courteous. He loved Sir Ector and his wife, and called them Father and Mother, for he thought that they were truly his parents. Sir Kay he thought was his brother, and he was glad and proud that Kay, who had been made knight only a few months before, should be going to joust at the tournament.

Sir Ector, Sir Kay, and Arthur set off to go to the lists. On the way there Sir Kay found that his sword, which he had unbuckled the night before, had been left at the house. He had forgotten it!

"I pray you, Arthur, ride back to the house and fetch me my sword," he said to the boy beside him.

"Willingly!" answered Arthur, and turning his horse's head round, he rode swiftly back to fetch Kay's sword. But when he got to the house, he found the door locked, for all the women had gone to see the tournament.

Then Arthur was angry and dismayed, for he knew how disappointed his brother would be if he returned without his sword.

"I will ride to the churchyard, and take the sword from the stone there," he said to himself. "My brother Kay shall not be without a sword this day!"

So when he came to the churchyard Arthur leapt off his horse, and tied it to a post. Then he went to ask the men who guarded the sword if he might take it. But they were not there, for they, too, had gone to the tournament.

Then the boy ran to the stone, and took hold of the handle of the sword. He pulled at it fiercely, and lo and behold! it came forth from the steel anvil, and shone brightly in the sunshine.

Arthur leapt on to his horse once again, and rode to Kay.

"Here is a sword for you, brother," he said.

Sir Kay took the beautiful weapon, and looked at it in amazement, for he knew at once that it was the sword from the stone. He ran to his father and showed it to him.

"Where did you get it?" asked Sir Ector, in astonishment and awe.

"My brother Arthur brought it to me," answered Sir Kay.

"Sir, I will tell you all," said Arthur, fearing that he had done wrong. "When I went back for Kay's sword I found the door locked. So, lest my brother should be without a weapon this day, I rode to the churchyard and took the sword from the great stone there."

"Then you must be king of this land," said Sir Ector, "for so say the letters around the anvil. Come with me to the churchyard, and you shall put the sword in the stone again and I will see you draw it forth."

The three rode to the church, and Arthur thrust the sword into the anvil, then drew it forth again easily and lightly. Then he put it back, and Sir Ector strove to draw it forth and could not. After him Sir Kay tried, but he could not so much as stir it an inch.

Then once again Arthur pulled it forth, and at that both Sir Ector and Sir Kay fell down upon their knees before him.

"Why do you kneel to me?" asked the boy. "My father and my brother, why is this?"

"Nay, nay," said Sir Ector. "We are not your father and your brother. Long years ago the magician Merlin brought you to us as a baby, and we took you and nursed you, not knowing who you were."

Then Arthur began to weep, for he was sad to hear that the man and woman he loved so much were not his parents, and that Kay was not his brother. But Sir Ector comforted him, and took him to the archbishop, bidding him tell how he had drawn forth the enchanted sword.

Then once again Arthur was bidden to ride to the churchyard, this time accompanied by all the lords and knights. He thrust the sword into the stone, and then pulled it forth. At that many lords came round the stone, shouting that what a mere boy could do could be done by a man with ease.

But when they tried to draw forth the sword, they could not. Each man had his turn, and failed. Then, before all the watching people, Arthur lightly drew out the sword, and flourished it around his head.

"We will have Arthur for our king!" shouted the people. "Let us crown him! He is our king, and we will have none other!"

Then they all knelt before him, and begged the archbishop to anoint him as king.

So, when the right time came, Arthur was crowned, and swore to be a true king, and to rule with justice all the days of his life.

The Round Table

After Arthur had been made king, many of his lords would not come to do him homage, and made war against him. The king fought bravely against them, and soon the kingdom was his from north to south, from east to west.

Then he set about making the country safe for honest men to live in. He captured robbers, slew wild beasts, and made wide paths through the gloomy forests so that men might journey here and there in peace and safety.

There was a king called Leodegrance whom Arthur helped greatly. This king had a fair daughter, Guinevere, and Arthur loved her as soon as he saw her. He sent to Leodegrance and asked him for his daughter's hand, which that king was pleased to grant.

Then in great pomp and ceremony the two were wed, and the lovely

Guinevere became Arthur's queen. Leodegrance sent Arthur a wonderful wedding present – the famous Round Table.

This had been made for King Uther Pendragon by Merlin the Magician. When Uther died, the table went to King Leodegrance, and he in his turn sent it to Arthur, who was full of joy to receive it.

It was a very large table, for it would seat one hundred and fifty knights. Leodegrance sent Arthur a hundred knights, and the king called Merlin to him, and bade him go forth into his kingdom and seek for fifty more true knights, worthy to sit at the Table.

Merlin set out, but he could find only twenty-eight, and these he brought back with him. Thus the table was not full, and there was always room for new knights. These were ordained at every Feast of Pentecost, and very proud were men or youths

when there came for them the great day on which they sat for the first time at the Round Table.

Merlin made the seats for the knights, and as soon as a knight had sat at the table, his name appeared in golden letters on his seat. Thus the knights always knew their places, and each man took his own.

Soon all the seats were full save only one, called the Siege Perilous, which no knight might take unless he was without any stain of sin. This was not filled until Sir Galahad came, for none dared sit there save him.

The greatest day in a knight's life was when he took upon himself the vows of true knighthood, and sat at the Round Table in the company of all the other noble knights. Then he had to swear to many things.

He must promise to obey the king; to show mercy to all who asked for it; to fight for the weak; to be kind, courteous, and gentle to all; and to do only those deeds which would bring honor and glory to knighthood.

So began the famous company of the Round Table, whose names have come down to us in many a brave and marvelous adventure. Any man or woman who was distressed could come to Arthur's court, sure of finding a knight who would ride forth and right their wrongs.

The Finding of the Sword Excalibur

King Arthur took a horse one morning, and set out to seek adventure. As he rode through the forest, he came to a fountain, and by it was a rich tent. A knight in full armor sat near by. He was tall, and very broad and strong. Never yet had he met a man who could defeat him in battle.

King Arthur made as if he would ride by, but the knight commanded him to stop.

"No knight passes here unless he first jousts with me," said the strange knight, Sir Pellinore.

"That is a bad custom," said Arthur. "No more must you joust here, Sir Knight."

"I take my commands from no man," answered the tall knight angrily. "If you would that I forswear this custom, then you must defeat me."

"I will do so!" said the king, and forthwith Sir Pellinore mounted his horse and the two rode at one another.

They met with such a shock that both their spears
were shivered to pieces on one another's shields. Then
Arthur pulled out his sword.

"Nay, not so," said the knight. "We will fight once
again with spears."

"I would do so, but I have no more," answered Arthur.

Then Sir Pellinore called his squire and bade him
bring two more spears. Arthur chose one and he took
the other. Then once again they rode at one another, and
for the second time they broke their spears. Then Arthur
set hand on his sword, but the knight stopped him.

"You are a passing good jouster," he said. "For the love
of the high order of knighthood, let us joust once again."

The squire brought out two great spears, and each
knight took one. Then they rode hard at one another,
and once more Arthur's spear was

broken. But Sir
Pellinore hit him so
hard in the middle of his
shield that he brought
both man and horse to
earth.

Then Arthur leapt to his

feet, and drew his sword.

"I will now fight you on foot, Sir Knight!" he cried, "for I have lost the honor on horseback."

So Sir Pellinore alighted, and the two set about one another with their swords. That was a great battle, and mighty were the strokes that each gave the other. Soon both were wounded, but they would not stop for that.

Then Arthur smote at Sir Pellinore just as the knight was smiting at him, and the two swords met together with a crash. Pellinore's was the heavier sword, and it broke the king's weapon into two pieces.

Arthur leapt straight at the knight, and taking him by the waist, threw him down to the ground. The knight, who was exceedingly strong rolled over on top of the king. Then he undid Arthur's helmet, and raised his sword to smite off his head.

But at that moment Merlin the Magician appeared, and cried out in a stern voice to Sir Pellinore:

"Hold your hand, Sir Knight, for he whom you are about to kill is a greater man than you know."

"Who is he?" asked the knight.

"He is King Arthur," answered Merlin.

"Then I must kill him for fear of his great wrath," cried Pellinore. He lifted up his sword, and was about to hew off the king's head, when Merlin cast an enchantment about him. His hand fell to his side, and he sank to the ground in a deep sleep. Then Merlin bade Arthur come with him, and the king, mounting on his horse, obeyed.

"You have not slain that knight by your enchantments?" asked Arthur anxiously. "He was a great knight, and strong and his only fault was his discourtesy."

"He will be quite whole again in three hours," said Merlin. "He is but cast into a sleep. There is not another knight in the kingdom so big and strong as he is. If he comes to crave your pardon, grant it, for he will do you good service."

Then Merlin took the king to a hermit, and the wise man tended Arthur's wounds, so that in three days he was ready to depart.

As they rode forth, Arthur glanced down at his side.

"I have no sword," he said, "Sir Pellinore broke mine in our battle."

"No matter," said Merlin. "You shall soon have another."

They rode on and came to a broad lake. In the midst a strange sight was to be seen; for out of the water came a hand and arm clothed in rich white silk, and in the hand was a beautiful sword that gleamed brightly.

"There is a sword for you," said Merlin. "See, it glitters yonder in the lake. Below the water is a wonderful palace, belonging to the Lady of the Lake, and it is she who has wrought this sword for you. Go, fetch it."

The king saw a little boat by the side of the lake, and

he untied it, and rowed on the water. When he came to the hand, he reached out and took the sword from it. As soon as he had done so the hand and arm disappeared under the water.

Arthur rowed back to land, and then, taking the sword from its scabbard, he looked at it closely. It was very beautiful, and the king was proud to have such a noble weapon. On each side were written mystic words that Arthur did not understand.

"What mean these writings?" he asked.

"On this side is written, 'Keep me,' and on the other, 'Throw me away,'" said Merlin. "But the time is far distant when you must throw it away. Look well at the scabbard. Do you like it or the sword the better of the two?"

"The sword," answered the king.

"You are unwise," said Merlin. "The scabbard is worth ten of the sword, for while you have the scabbard you will never lose blood, however sorely you may be wounded. So guard the scabbard well. The sword is called Excalibur, and is the best in the world."

Arthur rode back to his court with Merlin, glad to have such a fine weapon at his side. Joyfully his knights welcomed him into their company again, and once more they sat down together at the Round Table.

Before long Sir Pellinore came to crave pardon of the king for his discourtesy. Freely Arthur forgave him, and henceforth the great knight served the king well and faithfully, doing brave deeds in his service.

Balin, the Knight of the Two Swords

King Rience of North Wales once sent an insolent message to King Arthur:

"Eleven kings have I defeated, and their beards make a fringe for my mantle. There is yet a space for a twelfth, so with all speed send me yours, or I will lay waste your land from east to west."

The listening knights clapped their hands to their swords in anger, eager to slay the messenger, but the king forbade them.

"Get you gone!" he commanded the man sternly.

Now there was a knight there called Balin, he who wore two swords. He was very wrath when he heard the wicked message sent by King Rience, and he vowed to avenge the insult done to Arthur.

For eighteen months Balin had been in prison for slaying a knight of Arthur's court, and he longed to do some deed that would win him the king's favor once more. So he left the hall and went to don his armor, eager to fight against King Rience.

Whilst he was arming himself, a false lady came to the hall, and reminded the king that she had once done him a service.

"In return for the good I did you, I beg you to grant

me a favor," she said.

"Speak on," said the King.

"Give me the head of the knight Balin," said the lady.

"That I cannot do with honor," answered Arthur. "I pray you, madam, ask some other thing."

But the lady would not, and departed from the hall, speaking bitterly against the king. At the door she met the knight Balin, who was returning, fully armed.

As soon as he saw her, he rode straight at her and cut off her head, for he knew her to be a witch-woman and very wicked. She had caused his mother's death, and for three years he had sought for her in vain.

Then he rode forth to go against King Rience. But when Arthur found that he had cut off the lady's head, he was very angry.

"No matter what cause for anger he had against her, he should not have done such a thing in my court," said the king. "Balin has shamed us all. Sir Lanceor, ride after him and bring him back again."

Lanceor at once armed himself, and rode after Balin. He galloped his horse hard, and when he came up to Balin he shouted loudly – for he was an insolent knight – well pleased at the thought that Balin must needs go back with him to court.

"Stay, knight! You must stop whether you will or no, and I warrant your shield will not protect you if you turn to do battle with me!" he cried.

"What do you wish?" asked Balin fiercely, reining in his horse. "Would you joust with me, insolent knight? Have a care to yourself then!"

They rushed at one another with their spears held ready, and the two horses met with a crash. Lanceor's spear struck sideways on Balin's shield, and shivered to pieces, but Balin's spear ran right through the insolent knight's shield and slew him.

Balin looked sorrowfully at the knight, for he was sad to see a brave man fallen. He buried him, and went on his way grieving.

Soon he saw a knight riding towards him in the forest, and by the arms he bore he knew him to be his well-loved brother, Balan. They rode eagerly to meet one another, and greeted each other with joy.

"Now am I glad to see you," said Balan. "A man told me that you had been freed from your imprisonment, and I came to see you at the court."

"I go to avenge my lord Arthur," said Balin. "King Rience has done him an insult. Come with me, my brother, and together we will follow this adventure."

The two knights rode on side by side, and presently they met the magician Merlin.

"You ride to find King Rience," said Merlin, who knew the thoughts of all men. "Let me give you good counsel, and you shall meet with him and overcome him."

"We will do as you say," said Balin, and he and his brother followed the magician to a hiding-place in the wood, just beside a pathway.

"The king will come this way shortly with sixty knights," said Merlin.

It came to pass as the magician had said. King Rience rode by with his knights, and, when he came near, Balin and Balan rose up and attacked the company.

First they unhorsed King Rience, and struck him to the ground, where he lay wounded sorely. Then they rode at the rest of the knights, and so fiercely did the two brothers fight that soon forty of the king's men were vanquished, and the rest fled.

Then Balin returned to Rience, and would have slain

him, but he begged for mercy. So his life was spared, and
Balin and Balan took him to Arthur's court, and there
delivered him to the king to do with as he thought best.

Then the two brothers parted, and each went on his
way alone.

Balin met with strange adventures, and fought many
hard battles. Then one day as he rode onward, he came
to a cross, and on it, written in letters of gold, were these
words:

"It is perilous for a knight to ride alone towards this castle."

As he was reading this, Balin saw an old man coming
towards him, and heard him speak to him in warning.

"Balin of the Two Swords," he said, "do not pass this
way. Turn back, or you will ride into great peril."

When he had finished speaking he vanished. Then
Balin heard a horn blow as if some beast had been killed
in the hunt, and his blood turned cold within him.

"That blast was blown for me," said the knight. "I am
the beast who shall die – but I am still alive, and I will go
forward as befits a brave knight."

So he rode onwards past the cross, and soon came to
the castle. There he was welcomed by many fair ladies
and knights who led him into the castle and feasted him
royally.

Then the chief lady of the castle came to him and said:
"Sir Knight of the Two Swords, know that all knights

who pass this way must joust with one nearby who guards an island. No man may pass without so doing."

"That is an unhappy custom," said Balin; "but though my horse is weary my heart is not, and I will joust with this knight."

Then a man came up to Balin, and took his shield.

"Sir," he said, "your shield is not whole. Let me lend you mine, I pray you."

Balin agreed, and took the strange knight's shield instead of his own, which had his arms blazoned on. Then he mounted his horse and rode to where a great boat waited to take him and his charger to the island.

When he arrived at the island he met a maiden, and she spoke to him in dolorous tones.

"O Knight Balin, why have you left your own shield behind? You have put yourself in great danger by so doing."

"That I cannot help," said Balin, "for it is too late now to turn back. I must face what lies before me, for I am a knight of Arthur's court."

Then Balin heard the sound of hoofs, and saw a knight come riding out of a castle, clad in red armor, and his horse in trappings of the same color. When this knight saw Balin he thought that surely it must be his brother Balin, because he carried two swords – for the Red Knight was no other than Balan, who had been forced by a foe to keep the castle against all comers.

But when Balan looked upon his enemy's shield, he saw that it did not bear his brother's arms, and he therefore galloped straight at him, deeming him to be a stranger.

The two knights met with a fearful shock, and the spear of each smote the other down. They lay in a swoon upon the ground, and for some time they could not rise.

Then Balan leapt up, and went towards Balin, who arose to meet him. But Balan struck first, and his sword went right through his brother's shield, and smote his helmet. Then Balin struck back and felled his brother to the ground.

So they fought together till they had no more strength left, and each had seven great wounds. Then Balan laid himself down for a little, and Balin spoke to hm.

"What knight are you?" he said. "Never till now did I meet a knight that was my match."

"My name is Balan," answered the knight. "And I am brother to the good knight Balin of the Two Swords."

"Alas, that ever I should see this day!" cried Balin, in grief and dismay, for he loved his brother better than anyone else on earth. Then he fell in a faint.

Balan went to him and raised his helmet so that he might look upon his face. And when he saw that it was his own well-loved brother, he wept bitterly.

"Now when I saw your two swords I did indeed think you were my brother," he said, "but when I looked upon your shield and saw that it was not yours, I did not know you."

"A knight bade me take his in exchange for mine that was not whole," said Balin. "Great woe has he brought us this day, for we have slain one another, and the world will speak ill of us both for that!"

Then came the lady of the castle and her men. She wept to hear their tale, and when the two brothers begged her to bury them in the same grave, she promised with tears that she would do so.

So died Balin and Balan, and were buried in the same place. The lady knew Balan's name, but not Balin's, and she put above their grave how that the knight Balan was slain by his brother.

Then the next day came Merlin the Magician, and sorrowfully, in letters of gold, he wrote Balin's name there too. Then below he put the story of their deaths, that all men might know how it came to pass that the two brothers had each killed the other.

Prince Geraint and the Sparrowhawk

One morning the king and all his court went hunting. As soon as dawn came, there arose a great noise of baying hounds, of trampling feet, and thudding hoofs – the knights were getting to horse.

Queen Guinevere meant to ride with the huntsmen, but she slept late, and when she rose the sun was already high. She went with one of her ladies to a little hill from where she could see the hunt passing by.

As she waited there, Prince Geraint came riding to greet her. He too had slept late. He was not dressed for the hunt, but was clad in a surcoat of white satin, hung with a purple scarf.

He greeted the queen, and together they waited for the hunt to pass by. As they sat there on their horses, they saw some strangers riding near. There was a knight, fully armed, a lady with him, and behind them a misshapen, evil-faced servant.

"Who is yonder knight?" wondered the queen. She turned to her maiden, and bade her go and ask. The lady rode off, and prayed the servant to tell her his master's name.

"I will not tell you," answered the servant rudely.

"Then I will ask your master himself," said the maiden.

"You shall not!" cried the servant in anger, and struck the maiden across the face with his whip. She rode back to the queen in dismay and told her what had happened.

"This servant has insulted your maiden and you!" cried Prince Geraint in rage. "I will do your errand myself!"

He rode after the servant, and demanded his master's name. The ugly little servant refused to tell him, and when Geraint would have ridden to the knight himself to ask, the servant struck the prince such a blow across the mouth that the blood spurted forth, and stained his scarf.

Geraint clapped his hand to his sword, thinking to have slain him, but then, seeing that he was but a poor misshapen man, he stayed his anger. He rode swiftly back to the queen, and told her that he would ride after the knight, demand his name, and ask for redress for the wrong done to the queen and her maiden.

"I have no armor," he said, "but that I will perchance get at the next town. Farewell, madam. I go to ride after the churlish knight."

Geraint galloped after the knight, the lady, and the servant, and followed them closely all that day. Up hill and down they went, and towards evening they came to a town. They rode through the streets, and Geraint saw that all the people ran to watch them pass by, leaning out of windows to see them, and peering out of doorways.

The three travelers rode to a castle at the farther end of

the town, and entered the gates, which closed behind them.

"They will ride no further tonight," said Geraint. "I will find a lodging for myself, and buy armor so that I may challenge the knight on the morrow."

But no matter where Geraint went, people seemed too busy even to answer his questions. To his request for arms, he could only get the reply, "The Sparrowhawk, the Sparrowhawk," and this strange name seemed to be on the lips of everyone.

The town was full of people, and everywhere the smiths were polishing armor and sharpening swords. But for all the wealth of arms, there were none for Geraint.

"The Sparrow-hawk," answered an old man, who was busy pol-ishing a shield, when Geraint asked him for help. "Have you forgotten the Sparrowhawk? You will get no arms in this town tonight because of the Sparrowhawk."

"Who is this Sparrowhawk?" demanded Geraint impatiently, but no one could find time to answer him. He rode through the town, and at last, despairing of finding a lodging, came to a marble bridge that led to a half-ruined castle. On the bridge sat an old man, in rags that had once been rich clothing. He greeted Geraint courteously.

"Sir," said the prince, "can you tell me where I may get shelter for the night?"

"Come with me, and you shall have the best that my castle can offer," said the old man. He led Geraint to his castle, which the prince saw had been half burnt down. He took him inside, and seated by the fire Geraint saw the old man's wife and his daughter, Enid, the fairest maiden that the prince had ever seen. She was dressed in old and faded garments, but even these could not hide her loveliness.

"Enid," said the old man, "take the knight's horse to the stable, and then go into the town to buy bread and meat."

Geraint did not wish the maiden to do this errand for him, but she obeyed her father, and went. Soon she came back again, and set the supper for her father and his guest. She waited on them as they ate, and Geraint thought he had never before seen such a sweet and modest maiden.

"Why is your castle ruined like this?" the knight asked the old man.

"It is because of my nephew, the knight called the Sparrowhawk," said his host. "Three years ago he burnt my castle down because I would not give him my daughter Enid for his wife. I am Earl Yniol, and once all this broad earldom was mine; but now I have barely enough left of my great wealth to show kindness to strangers like yourself. The Sparrowhawk lives in the big castle yonder, and, as you saw, the whole town is in a ferment about him."

"Why is that?" asked Geraint. "I could not get arms as I rode through, for every one murmured 'The Sparrowhawk! Have you forgotten the Sparrowhawk?'"

"He holds his yearly tournament tomorrow," said the earl. "On the field is set up a silver rod, on which is placed a silver sparrowhawk. My nephew challenges all knights to win this prize from him. Two years has he won it, and when he wins it the third time, as he will, I fear, it becomes his for always, and all men will know him as the Sparrowhawk."

"This Sparrowhawk must be the knight who this morning insulted the queen and her maiden," said Geraint. "I will challenge him tomorrow, if only I can get some arms."

"I have arms," said Earl Yniol. "But they are old and rusty. Even so, Sir Knight, you cannot enter the lists tomorrow, for only they that have ladies to fight for, and proclaim them to be the fairest there, may enter the tournament."

"Lord Yniol," cried Geraint, "let me fight for your daughter Enid, for surely she is the fairest maiden in the land! If I win, I will marry her, and she shall be my true wife."

The earl was proud to think that such a famous knight as Geraint should ask for his daughter's hand.

"If Enid consents, you shall have your wish," he said. "Now we must seek our beds, for tomorrow you must arise early if you would enter the tournament."

Next day Geraint donned the rusty armor that the earl found for him, and rode to the lists. Yniol, his wife and their daughter Enid went to watch the tournament, praying that the brave prince would be the victor.

The Sparrowhawk rode proudly on to the field, while all the heralds blew loudly on their trumpets. He called to his lady, and pointed to the silver sparrowhawk on the rod.

"Take it, lady," he said. "It is yours, for no maiden here is fairer than you."

"Stay!" cried Geraint, galloping up. "Here is a lovelier maiden, and for her I claim the silver sparrowhawk!"

The surprised knight looked at Geraint, and then, seeing his old and rusty armor, laughed mockingly.

"Do battle for it!" he cried.

Then he and the prince rode at one another with their lances in rest. So fiercely did they come together that each broke his spear. Again and again they galloped on one another, and then Geraint rode at the Sparrowhawk with such fury that he smote him from his horse, and he fell to the ground, saddle and all.

Then the two set upon one another with their swords, and the sparks flew as the hard steel met.

They fought fiercely, till Geraint raised his sword, and smote the other on the helmet. The sharp weapon cleft right through it, and cut to the bone. The Sparrowhawk dropped his sword and fell to the ground.

"I surrender," he said weakly.

"Tell me your name," demanded Geraint.

"Edyrn, son of Nudd," replied the vanquished knight. "Spare my life, I pray you."

"On this condition," said Geraint sternly. "You shall return to the earl all that you robbed him of, and you shall go to Arthur's court, and there crave pardon for your sins."

"I will do this," promised the Sparrowhawk. "Let me go now, I beg you, for my wounds are heavy."

Geraint dragged him to his feet, and he went to have his wounds dressed. Then proudly the prince took the silver sparrowhawk from its rod and gave it to Enid. Bitter were the real Sparrowhawk's thoughts, as he saw Geraint place it in the hands of the maiden he would dearly love to have married.

"Tomorrow, fair Enid, you shall ride with me to Arthur's court, and there we will be wed," said Geraint.

That night there was merry feasting in Earl Yniol's castle, for Edyrn, his nephew, had returned to him his wealth, and many of the townspeople had brought back to the castle treasure that had been taken three years before.

The next day the earl brought Enid to the prince, dressed in a lovely gown that her mother had found for her. But Geraint wanted her in her old faded dress.

"Go, I pray you, and put on the gown you wore when

first I saw you," he said. "I would bring you to the queen in that robe, and she shall dress you in garments bright as the sun for your wedding."

Enid obeyed, for she wished to wear the dress in which Geraint loved her best. Then happily they set off for Caerleon, and soon arrived at the court.

Queen Guinevere kissed the shy and lovely maiden, and with her own fair hands she dressed her for her wedding. Everyone loved her, and Geraint most of all.

When they were married they lived for many months at the court, and were as happy as prince and lady could be. Soon there came riding Edyrn, the Sparrowhawk, coming to crave pardon for his evil deeds. Freely Arthur forgave him, and sent him forth to do battle for him against wicked and pestilent men.

In time he became a good and true knight, and won for himself a great name in fighting for the king.

The Further Adventures of Geraint and Enid

For a year Geraint and Enid lived at Arthur's court. Enid was loved by all, for she was gentle and kind, and Geraint was the foremost knight in every tournament, brave, handsome, and strong.

But soon there came news to Geraint of robbers in his own land of Devon. He went to Arthur and begged leave to return to his home, to fight the robbers and put them all to flight, so that once again honest men might travel without fear.

The king gave his consent, and Geraint and Enid set forth. When he came to Devon, Geraint rode out to destroy the bands of robbers. Soon he had driven them forth, and once more his country was at peace.

But when he had done that, Geraint seemed to forget that there were such things as hunts and tournaments. He loved Enid so much that he wished always to be with her, and would never leave her side. He would not go hunting, and he would no longer ride to tournaments, so that the nobles spoke his name mockingly, and the common people called him coward.

Enid heard of this, and she was grieved, for she could not bear to think that because of her Geraint was called coward. She did not dare to tell him what she had heard, but daily she grew sadder, and at last the prince became uneasy, not knowing the reason for her pale, unhappy face.

One summer morning Enid awoke early and gazed upon Geraint as he lay sleeping. So huge he looked, and so strong, that Enid wept to think that because of her he had become weak, and would not play the part of a man.

"Alas, alas!" she said, "how grievous it is that I should be the cause of my lord's shame! If I were a true wife to him, I should tell him all that is in my heart."

At that moment Geraint awoke, and heard her words. He thought that she was reproaching herself because she no longer loved him, and was weary of being with him. He wondered, too, if she scorned him for proving himself so poor a knight of late. He asked her nothing, but in anger he called to his squire, and ordered him to get ready his horse and Enid's palfrey.

"Put on your oldest clothes," he said to the astonished girl. "You shall ride with me into the wilderness. I will show you that I am still as brave a knight as when I fought the Sparrowhawk, and won the prize for you."

"Why do you say this?" asked Enid.

"Ask me no questions," answered Geraint sternly.

Enid went to find her meanest clothes, and remembered the old, faded dress in which Geraint had first seen and loved her. She clad herself in it, thinking that

perhaps, when the prince saw her thus gowned, he
would remember too, and be gentle to her.

Soon the squire brought their horses,
and they mounted.

"Ride before me," said Geraint to Enid.
"And do not turn back
nor speak to me, no
matter what you see
or hear, for I would
have no speech
with you this day."

So Enid rode
sadly in front.
Soon they came to
a vast and lonely
forest, and there, as she rode, Enid saw four armed men
hiding some way ahead.

"See," said one; "here comes a doleful knight. We shall
find it easy to overcome him, and then we will take his
arms and his lady."

Enid heard these words, and was fearful, for she did
not know if Geraint would see the men. Yet she was
afraid to ride back and tell him, for she thought he
would be angry with her.

"Still, I would rather he stormed at me, or even killed
me, than that he should be set upon and slain by these
robbers," she thought.

So she waited until Geraint came up to her, and then she told him of the men ahead.

"Did I not say that you were to speak no word to me?" said Geraint in anger. Then he rode furiously at the four robbers, who came to meet him. He used such force that his spear entered the body of the first robber, and went right through it. He did the same to the second, but the third and the fourth, seeing his great strength, turned their horses aside, and fled for their lives.

But they could not escape Geraint. He rode after them, and slew them both. Then he stripped all the dead robbers of their armor, tied it upon their horses, and knotted the bridle reins together. He gave the reins to Enid, and bade her drive the four horses in front of her.

"And speak to me again at your peril!" he siad sternly.

Enid took the reins, and went forward as she was bidden, happy that her lord was safe. After some while her ears caught the sound of hoofs, and through the trees she saw three horsemen riding. Their voices came to her clearly.

"Good fortune is ours today!" said one. "See, here come four horses with armor tied upon them, and only one knight to guard them."

"And he is a coward, surely," said another. "See how he hangs his craven head!"

Enid knew that Geraint was weary with his last fight, and she resolved to warn him, even though he might punish her for speaking. So again she waited until he came up to her, and then spoke.

"I see three men, lord," she said. "They mean to take your booty for themselves."

"I would rather be set upon by three men than have your disobedience!" cried Geraint wrathfully. Then, seeing that the horsemen were almost upon him, he rode fiercely at the foremost and smote him straight from his horse. Then he slew the other two with mighty strokes, and dismounting, he stripped them of their armor in the same manner as before, and tied it upon the horses.

Now Enid had seven horses to drive before her, and she found her task difficult. Geraint was sad at heart to see his lady labor so, but he was stubborn of temper, and said nothing. They passed out from the gloomy forest, and came to open hills and fields, where reapers were at work.

Seeing that Enid was faint with hunger, Geraint beckoned to a boy who was taking dinner to the reapers. He carried bread and meat, and gaped to see such a fine knight, with a lady driving seven horses laden with armor.

"Give the lady some of the food you carry," commanded Geraint. "She is faint."

"Gladly, Sir Knight!" said the boy. "See, I will spread all I have before you, for I can go back to the town and fetch more for the reapers."

So he spread out the bread and meat, and watched Geraint and Enid eat. When they had finished he took up the remains, and put them into his basket, saying that he would now return to the town for fresh food.

"Do so," said Geraint, "and find a fair lodging there for myself and the lady. In return for your service, you may take a horse and armor for yourself. Choose which you will from among the seven."

The boy was beside himself with joy. He chose a horse

and armor, and leapt up on his steed. Then, thinking himself already a knight, he rode off to the town.

Geraint and Enid followed. They came to an inn, in which the biggest room was set ready for them. Suddenly there arose the sound of loud voices and tramping hoofs. Then into the inn strode the lord of that country, the Earl of Doorn, with twelve of his followers.

Geraint greeted him, and he Geraint. Then they ordered the host of the inn to set out a fine meal, and all of them sat down to feast. Geraint took no notice of

Enid, who sat in the furthest corner, hoping that no one would notice her. But the earl saw her, and thought she was very lovely.

After the feast was over, he went to Enid and spoke to her.

"Why do you go with your knight?" he asked. "He is churlish to you, and treats you shamefully. Why does he let you travel without page or maiden to wait upon you? He is truly a discourteous knight."

"Not so," answered Enid loyally. "He is my lord, and I go willingly with him wheresoever he wishes."

"Say but the word, and I will have him slain," said the earl. "We are many, and he is but one. Then you shall come with me, and share my fair lands and my great riches."

"No," said Enid. "That I cannot do, for I love my lord, and will not leave him."

"What if I kill him, and take you with me, whether you will or no!" said the wicked knight.

Enid was filled with terror, for she saw that the earl would do what he said. So she answered guilefully:

"Nay, take me not by force. Come tomorrow, for I am too weary now to ride with you. Then you shall slay my lord, and I will come with you willingly."

The earl promised to come the next day, and rode off with his followers. Geraint flung himself down on a couch and fell fast asleep, but Enid stayed awake, watching fearfully, dreading lest the earl should come during the night.

When dawn was near she put ready Geraint's armor, and awoke him.

"Arm yourself, my lord," she said, "for you must save both yourself and me also."

Then she told him what the wicked earl had said to her, and though Geraint reproached her angrily for speaking to him again, he hastily armed himself, and called for their horses. In payment for his night's lodging, he left the six horses and armor, and the host of the inn could hardly believe in his great good fortune.

They had not been gone from the inn very long when the wicked Earl of Doorn came hammering at the door with forty men at his back. When he heard that Geraint had gone, he was very angry, and at once galloped down the road that the prince had taken.

Soon Enid's quick ears caught the sound of pursuing hoofs, and she turned.

"My lord," she cried to Geraint, "do you not see the earl and his men riding down upon us?"

"Yes, I see them," replied Geraint in wrath; " and I see also that you will never obey me!"

The prince turned his horse, and rode straight at the earl. So violently did he meet him that his foe was flung right off his horse, and lay on the ground as if dead. Then Geraint rode at the men behind, unhorsed many, and wounded others so badly that the rest fled in fear, terrified at their master's overthrow.

Seeing that his enemies were all slain or fled, Geraint signed to Enid to ride on. For about an hour they traveled forward in the hot summer sun. Then, suddenly, without warning, Geraint pitched forward on his horse, and fell heavily to the ground. He had received a sore wound in his last fight, and it had bled under his armor. The knight had fainted, and now lay prone in the highway.

In alarm Enid dismounted and ran to him. She loosened his armor and tried to stop the wound with her veil. She took his head on her lap, and, leaning over him, sheltered him from the burning sun, for she was not strong enough to drag him into the shade.

Presently a troop of horsemen came that way, with the Earl Limours at their head.

The earl stopped and looked at Enid as she sat weeping.

"Is your knight slain?" he asked. "Do not weep for him, fair lady, but come with me, and I will treat you well."

"He is not dead!" said Enid, weeping still more bitterly. "Oh, Sir Knight, help me to take him to some place of shelter, where I may tend him well."

"He is surely dead," said the earl. "But for the sake of your fair face, I will carry him to my castle."

Two servants picked Geraint up. Enid mounted her palfrey, and the troop moved off once more. Soon they reached the earl's castle. Geraint was placed on a couch, and Enid knelt by him, trying to bring him back to life by all the means in her power.

And soon Geraint recovered a little, for he was not dead. But he still lay in a kind of swoon, hearing what passed around him, but thinking it to be part of a dream.

The earl commanded a feast to be set ready, for he was hungry. Presently the table was spread with foods of all kinds, and the earl and his men sat down to the meal. After a while the earl remembered the fair lady whose knight he had brought to the castle, and he looked round for her.

"Leave your dead knight!" he called. "Come and sit by

me, and you shall be my lady!"

"I will neither eat nor drink till my lord eats with me," said Enid.

"You speak rashly," said Earl Limours. "You shall obey me, and drink."

He filled a goblet with wine, and went to where poor Enid crouched in terror.

"Drink!" he commanded.

"Be pitiful!" begged Enid. "Leave me to my sick lord."

Then the earl, full of rage, struck her across the face with his hand. Enid, thinking that her lord must indeed be dead, or the earl would never dare to do such a cruel thing, gave a loud and grievous cry.

The sound awoke Geraint from his swoon, and with sudden strength he leapt from his couch. He threw himself upon the Earl Limours, and with one blow cut his head clean off. All the rest of the people fled screaming from the hall, for they thought that a dead man had come to life.

Then Geraint turned to Enid, and looked with love and sorrow upon her.

"I had thought that you did not love me," he said, "but I did you great wrong, and I crave your pardon."

They kissed one another, but Enid was full of fear lest the earl's men should return.

"Let us fly while there is yet time, my lord," she begged. "Your charger is outside. Let us go quickly."

She took Geraint to where his horse stood by the gate, and he mounted it, with Enid set behind him. Then together they rode off to Geraint's castle, happy once again.

And never more did Geraint doubt his lady, nor did Enid have cause to sigh that men spoke mockingly of her lord – for Geraint was ever foremost in hunt, battle, and tournament, and all men spoke his name with love and honor.

Gareth, the Knight of the Kitchen

It was Arthur's custom at the Feast of Pentecost not to sit down to meat until he had seen some strange sight. There came a year when he held the feast at Kin-Kenadonne, and before he went to eat he looked about for some strange thing.

Then Sir Gawaine glanced through a window, and saw three men on horseback, and a servant afoot. The men alighted, and one of them was higher than the others by a foot and a half. They walked towards the king's hall, and the tall young man leaned heavily on the shoulders of the others as if he would hide his great stature and strength.

He was very handsome, and very broad of shoulder. His hands were fair and large, and very strong. When he saw King Arthur sitting on his throne he went up to him, and stood up straight and tall.

"King Arthur," said the youth, "God bless you and all your fair fellowship of the Round Table. I am come hither to ask three favors of you. The first I will ask now, the second and third a year hence."

"Ask, and you shall have your wish," said Arthur, liking the youth greatly.

"Grant that I may have food and drink for a twelvemonth," said the youth.

"Ask something better," said Arthur. "You may have it for the asking."

"I want nothing more," said the youth.

"So be it," said the king. "You shall have the food and drink you want. Now tell me your name."

"I cannot tell you that," said the youth.

"That is strange!" said Arthur. "You are the goodliest young man that ever I saw, and yet you cannot tell your name! Ho, Sir Kay! Where is Sir Kay, my steward? Bid him see that this youth has good food and drink, and is treated like a lord's son, for I like his looks very well."

"Like a lord's son!" said the churlish Sir Kay. "That were folly indeed! If he had been of high birth, then would he have asked for a horse and armor, and not for food and drink. He is a common serving-boy, and none other! He shall live in the kitchen with the other serving-lads, and eat with them. And since he cannot tell his name, I will give him one. He shall be called Fairhands, for never did I see a serving-boy with such white hands as his!"

Sir Gawaine and Sir Lancelot were angry at Sir Kay's mockery, and bade him cease his jibes. But Sir Kay took no heed of them.

"Come with me to the kitchen, Fairhands!" he commanded. "There shall you have fat broth every day, and in a year's time you will be as fat as a pork-hog!"

The youth went to the kitchen, and sat with the kitchen-lads, who jeered at him. But when they saw his angry strength, they grew afraid. Only Sir Kay mocked at him openly, and gave him the worst and the dirtiest work to do.

Fairhands did not complain, but did as he was bid. Sir Gawaine and Sir Lancelot would have had him come to their rooms for meat and drink, but he would not. He stayed with the kitchen-lads, ate with them, and slept on the kitchen floor with them at night.

But whenever there was any jousting among the knights, Fairhands was there, looking on eagerly; and when there were games of skill between the kitchen-boys, he always beat the rest with ease; and often Sir Lancelot would look at him, and wonder who and what he was.

At last the year was up, and the Feast of Pentecost came again. As the king was sitting at meat, there came a damsel into the hall, asking to speak with him.

"Sir," she said, "I am the Lady Lynette, and I come to your court for help."

"What is your trouble?" asked the king.

"I come to beg your help on behalf of a great lady," said the damsel. "She is besieged in her castle by a tyrant knight, who will not let her go forth. Will you send one of your noble knights to rescue her?"

"What is the lady's name?" asked the king. "Where does she dwell, and who is the knight that besieges her?"

"The wicked knight is called the Red Knight of the Red Lands," answered the damsel. "As for the lady's name, that may I not tell you."

"None of my knights can go with you if you cannot tell the lady's name, nor where she dwells," said Arthur.

But as he spoke, Fairhands came forward and stood before the king.

"Sir King," he said, "I have been for twelve months in your kitchen, and I thank you for my food and drink. Now I crave leave to ask my two further favors."

"Speak on," said Arthur.

"Sir," said the youth, "I pray you to let me have the adventure of this damsel. My second favor is that you will let Sir Lancelot ride after me and make me knight, if he thinks I am worthy."

"Your requests are granted," said the king.

But the damsel was very angry when she heard that Fairhands was to be her knight.

"Fie, fie!" she cried. "Am I to have none but a kitchen-page?"

She ran to her horse and mounted in rage. Then she rode away swiftly, but Fairhands saw the way she went.

At that moment a messenger came to the youth, and told him that his horse and armor had come for him. At that every one was astonished, and went to see what manner of arms the kitchen-boy had. Outside they saw a servant, and with him he had a goodly horse and a fine suit of armor.

Then Fairhands armed himself quickly, and when he came into the hall to bid the king farewell, there was hardly a knight there that looked as noble as he. He took leave of the king, and then rode swiftly to join the damsel.

Everyone looked after him, and Sir Kay was angry to think that his kitchen-boy was gone.

"I will ride after him and see if he knows his kitchen-master!" he cried. So he leapt to horse, and rode up to Fairhands, crying to him to stop.

"Do you not know me, your master?" he said.

Fairhands turned and saw him.

"Yes, I know you well," he answered. "You are the most ungentle knight of all the court!"

With that he rode straight at Sir Kay and unhorsed him, giving him a sore wound as he did so. Sir Kay fell to the ground and lay as if he were dead. Then up rode Sir Lancelot, and Fairhands called upon him to joust with him.

So the two rode at one another fiercely, and met with such a shock that each fell to earth. Then they fought together with swords, and Sir Lancelot marveled at the youth, for he was so big and strong that he fought more like a giant than a man. At last Sir Lancelot began to feel that Fairhands might press him too hard, and he cried out to him: "Fairhands, do not fight so hard, for we have no quarrel, as you know. We are but jousting."

"That is true," said Fairhands. "But, my lord, it is good to feel my strength against yours. Tell me, am I worthy yet to be made knight?"

"You are very worthy," said Sir Lancelot. "Kneel before me, and tell me your name, and I will knight you here and now."

"Keep my secret, I pray you," said Fairhands, kneeling down. "My name is Gareth, and I am a son of King Lot of Orkney. Sir Gawaine is my brother."

"I am glad of that," said Sir Lancelot. "I guessed that

you were of princely birth."

Then he knighted Gareth, and bade him keep well the order of knighthood. Sir Gareth rose up, mounted his horse, and with a heart full of gladness rode after the damsel.

Sir Gareth Goes Adventuring

When the Lady Lynette saw him coming, she turned to him angrily.

"Why do you come after me?" she said. "You smell of the kitchen! You are but a serving-lad and a dish-washer!"

"Say what you will," said Gareth. "I go with you, for so I have promised King Arthur, and I must follow this adventure to the end."

Now as they rode, a man came running out from the trees, and sped to Gareth's side.

"Lord, lord, help me!" he cried. "My master has been captured by six thieves, and they have bound him. I fear he will be slain."

"Take me to him," commanded Gareth.

He followed the man, and soon came to where the six robbers were. Gareth rode straight into them, struck the first one dead, and then the second. The he turned upon the third and slew him also. The others fled, but Gareth rode after them and smote them down. Then he returned to the bound knight and unloosed him.

"I give you great thanks," said the knight. "Now as night is coming fast, I pray you bring your lady to my castle hard by, and you shall sup with me and rest there till the morrow."

So Lynette and Gareth went to the castle, and there the knight commanded food and drink to be brought. But when he would have set the damsel and Gareth together at the table with him, Lynette was angry.

"Fie on you for a discourteous knight!" she said. "Would you have us sit at table with a kitchen-boy that smells of grease? He knows better how to kill a pig than to eat with a lady!"

Then the knight of the castle was ashamed to hear her unkind words. He bade his servants set a table apart, and to it he took Gareth and sat with him, talking merrily all the night through. But as for Lynette, she supped alone.

The next day Gareth and Lynette set out once more. Soon they came to a river, and there was but one place where it might be crossed. On the other side of the ford sat two knights, and they would let no one pass over the river.

"You had better turn back, kitchen-boy," said Lynette. "You are no match for two knights."

"If they were six I should still ride onward," answered Gareth. He rushed into the water, and one of the knights came to meet him. They broke their spears, and then drew their swords. Gareth smote the knight upon his head, and he fell into the water and was drowned.

Then Gareth spurred his horse up the bank on the farther side, where the second knight awaited him. Fiercely he fought him, and it was not long before he had cleft the other's helmet, and slain him outright.

But Lynette had no word of praise.

"Alas!" she said, "that two good knights should take their death from the hands of a common serving-lad! You did not fight fairly. The horse of the first knight stumbled, and threw him into the water, and you went behind the second knight and struck him a false blow."

"Say what you will, damsel, I follow this adventure," said Gareth.

Then on they rode again until they came to a black and desolate land. In front of them they saw a black hawthorn tree, and on it hung a black banner and a black shield. By it stood a black spear and a black horse, and on a black stone there sat a knight, armed all in black harness, who was the Knight of the Black Lands.

"Run while there is time!" said Lynette to Gareth mockingly. "See, here before us is a knight who will slay you with ease."

"Damsel," said the Black Knight, greeting her, "is this knight your champion?"

"Nay; he is not a knight," said Lynette. "He is but a common serving-boy from King Arthur's kitchen."

"Then I will not fight him," said the Black Knight. "I will take his horse and harness from him, and make him go afoot. It were shame to fight a poor kitchen-boy."

"You speak freely of my horse and harness," said Gareth wrathfully. "You must fight me for them before you get them! Look to yourself now!"

With that he rode headlong at the Black Knight, and
the two horses met with a sound like thunder. The Black
Knight's spear broke, and they drew their swords. They
hacked at one another fiercely, and each gave the other
sore wounds. But after an hour and a half the Black
Knight fell from his horse in a swoon and so died.

Then Gareth stripped the knight of his fine black harness,
and took it for himself, for it was better than his own. Then

he mounted the knight's horse, and rode after the damsel.

But still she would have none of him, and pushed him away from her, holding her nose daintily.

"Away, kitchen-knight, away!" she cried. "The smell of your clothes comes to me on the wind, and they smell strong of the kitchen. Alas, that such a fine knight should be slain by you! Soon you will meet one that shall punish you well, so I bid you flee away, while yet there is time."

"I may be beaten or slain," said Gareth, "but I will never flee away."

As they rode on another knight came towards them. He was all in green, both his horse and his harness. He rode up to the damsel and greeted her.

"Is that my brother, the Black Knight, who is with you?" he asked.

"Nay, nay," she answered; "this is but a kitchen knave, who has falsely slain your brother, and taken his horse and armor."

"Ah, traitor!" cried the Green Knight, turning fiercely on Gareth. "You shall die for slaying my brother!"

"I defy you!" said Gareth. "I did not slay your brother shamefully, but in fair fight."

Then they rode at one another, and both their spears broke. They drew their swords and began to fight furiously. Gareth's horse swerved into the Green Knight's horse, so that it fell, whereupon the knight slid lightly off, and attacked Gareth on foot. The youth at once leapt off his horse, and fought on foot also.

Suddenly the Green Knight smote such a mighty blow upon Gareth's shield that it cleft it right asunder. Then was Gareth ashamed, and he in turn gave him a buffet upon the helmet. So fierce a blow it was that the knight fell to the ground, and immediately begged for mercy.

"I will spare your life only if my damsel asks me," said Gareth, resolved to make Lynette crave something from him.

"False kitchen-page, I will never beg anything from you!" said Lynette.

"Then he shall die," said Gareth, and unlaced the Green Knight's helmet as if he would slay him.

"Nay, spare me!" pleaded the Green Knight in fear. "If you will grant me my life, I and my thirty men will be yours, and will follow you gladly, for you are a fierce and lusty fighter."

"Shame that a kitchen-boy should have you and your thirty good men for his followers!" cried Lynette in a rage.

"Damsel, speak a word for me," begged the Green Knight.

"Unless the lady prays me to spare your life, you shall die." said Gareth, and he raised his sword.

"Let be," said Lynette hastily. "You miserable kitchen-knave, let be."

"Damsel, I obey you," said Gareth, and he lowered his sword. "Sir Knight, I give you your life at this lady's request. Rise up."

Then the Green Knight kneeled himself at Gareth's feet and did him homage.

"Come to my castle, where I can do you honor," he said. "You shall feast with me, and rest there for the night."

So Lynette and Gareth followed him to his castle. But the damsel ever reproached Gareth, and would not sit at table with him. So the Green Knight took him to a table apart, and sat with him gladly.

"You do wrong, maiden, to reproach this noble knight in such manner," said he. "He is no kitchen-boy, but a fair and courteous knight."

Then for the first time Lynette was ashamed of the harsh words she spoke, for she knew well that Gareth had behaved in a true and knightly manner, and had never once answered her reproaches with angry words.

She turned to Gareth and begged his forgiveness.

"Pardon me, I pray you, for all I have said or done to you," she said.

"With all my heart I pardon you," said Gareth. "It gladdens me to hear you speak pleasant words, and now there is no knight living that is too strong for me, so happy am I in your pleasure."

When morning came, Gareth and Lynette set forth once more, riding together happily for the first time. They rode through a fair forest, and came to a plain on which was set a beautiful castle.

As they rode towards it Gareth saw a strange and dreadful sight, for upon great trees hung goodly armed knights, their shields about their necks. Gareth counted forty, and with a sad countenance he turned to Lynette and asked her how all the knights had met their death.

"Well may you look sad," said the damsel. "These forty knights are they that came to rescue my sister, Dame Lyonors. The Knight of the Red Lands, who now besieges her castle, defeated each one, and put them to the shameful death you see. Now haste you away while there is time, for the knight will treat you in the same manner."

But Gareth had no thought of turning back. He rode onwards with Lynette, and soon they came to the castle.

By it stood a great sycamore tree, and on a branch was hung a mighty horn of elephant's tusk.

"Any knight that comes hither to rescue my sister, Dame Lyonors, must blow this horn, and then the Knight of the Red Lands makes himself ready for battle," said Lynette.

Gareth spurred his horse eagerly, and rode up to the

tree. He blew the horn so loudly that the sound echoed for miles around.

The Red Knight of the Red Lands armed himself hastily, and rode out to meet Gareth. He was harnessed all in blood red, and he rode a red horse and carried a red spear.

"Yonder is your deadly enemy," said the damsel, turning pale. "And see, yonder too is my lovely sister, the Lady Lyonors, looking down on us from the castle."

Gareth looked up to see the lady, and as soon as he saw her sweet face, he felt his heart warm with love.

"She is the fairest lady ever I looked upon," he said.

"She shall be my love, and for her will I gladly fight."

Then the Red Knight called out in a loud voice:

"Cease your looking, Sir Knight, for she is my lady."

"That is a lie," said Gareth. "If she were your lady, I should not have come to rescue her from you. She loves you not. She shall be my lady, so make yourself ready to do battle for her."

Then the two rode at each other, with their spears in rest, and came together with such a mighty shock that both fell to the ground and lay there stunned. Those that looked on thought that each had broken his neck. But in a short time the two knights leapt up, put their shields before them, and ran against one another with their swords.

Then began a terrible battle, and soon each knight was sorely wounded, but neither would give in. For hours they hacked at one another, and then, when each was panting for breath, they lay down to rest.

Once again they ran together, hurtling forward as if they had been two rams. In places their armor was all hewn off, and their wounds bled sorely.

So the battle went on, until Gareth, glancing up to the

castle, saw the Lady Lyonors smiling down upon him with love in her eyes. Then he leapt to the fight with greater strength.

Suddenly the Red Knight struck him such a mighty blow that Gareth's sword flew from his hand, and he fell to earth. The Red Knight fell on top of him and held him down, striving to deal the death-blow.

Then loudly cried the maiden Lynette: "Oh, kitchen-knight, where is your courage? My sister weeps to see you so."

Her words stirred Gareth's heart, and with a great effort he rose up, leapt to his sword, and then turned once more upon the Red Knight. This time he struck his foe's sword from his hand, and when he saw the Red Knight lying on the ground, he leapt on him, and began to unlace his helmet to slay him.

"I yield, I yield!" cried the knight in a loud voice.

"You do not deserve your life," said Gareth sternly, "for you have put many good knights to a shameful death."

"I yield to your mercy!" cried the Red Knight again.

"I will release you on one condition," said Gareth at last. "You must go to the castle, and crave pardon of the Lady Lyonors for all your wrongdoing. If she forgives you, you may go free. After that you must go to King Arthur's court, and there humbly recite your evil deeds, and crave pardon of him too."

The Red Knight promised to do this, and Gareth freed him. When the Lady Lynette saw that the fight was over she hastened to Gareth and dressed his wounds. Then she had him carried into the castle, where the Lady Lyonors tended him lovingly.

Soon Gareth had won her promise to marry him, and when he returned to Arthur's court, she went with him to be wed. Then was King Arthur glad to know that the one-time kitchen-boy was no other than Prince Gareth, his own nephew. Proudly he listened to the many tales that his knights told him of Gareth's prowess and bravery.

Then the Lady Lyonors and Sir Gareth were wed with great pomp and honor, and happily did they live together at Arthur's court. As for the damsel Lynette, she came again to the court, and married Sir Gaheris, Gareth's younger brother. Then were they all happy, and lived at peace one with another.

The Bold Sir Peredur

There was once a great earl who had seven sons. Six of them went to tournaments with him, but the seventh was too young. Then one day there came news that the earl and his six strong sons had all been killed.

The poor mother was filled with grief. She had only one boy left now – Peredur, the youngest. She took him away to a lonely place, where dwelt only women and old men, and where he would never hear of knights and tournaments, arms and battle.

Peredur grew up straight and strong. He was happy among the hills and woods, and knew nothing of the world of knights and lords. Then one day Sir Owain, one of Arthur's own knights, came riding by. Peredur saw him, and stood still in the greatest amazement. What was this fine stranger, sitting grandly on a horse more beautiful than Peredur had ever seen before?

Sir Owain reined in his steed, and spoke to the boy.

"Have you seen a knight pass by this way?" he asked.

"A knight?" said Peredur. "I pray you, tell me what a knight may be."

"One like myself!" said Sir Owain, laughing.

Then Peredur felt the saddle with his strong fingers.

"What is this?" he asked, and the knight told him. Then the youth took hold of Sir Owain's sword and spear, and asked their names too, and what they were used for. The knight told him all he wanted to know, and then Peredur bade him farewell and ran off.

He went to where the horses were kept – gaunt, bony creatures used for carrying firewood – and picked the strongest out for himself. He placed a pack on the horse's back for a saddle, and then picked some supple twigs from which to make himself trappings such as he had seen upon Sir Owain's steed.

Then he went to say farewell to his mother, for he had resolved to be a knight like the man he had spoken to. The poor woman was full of distress, but she did not keep him back. Instead, she gave him some good advice.

"Ride to Arthur's court," she said, "for there you will find the noblest company of knights in the kingdom."

Peredur proudly rode off. He was a strange figure on his bony old horse. He held a long, sharp-pointed stick in his hand for a spear, and he thought gladly of the day when he would indeed be a knight.

After many days he came to Arthur's court. At the same moment there rode up an insolent knight, so vain of his strength and skill he was resolved to fight with anyone of the king's knights, and, by overthrowing him, gain glory and honor for himself.

This knight entered the hall in front of Peredur, and snatching up a goblet, threw the wine it contained straight into the face of Queen Guinevere.

"Does any knight here dare to avenge the insult I do the queen?" cried the arrogant knight. "If any one of you is bold enough to do battle with me, let him follow me to the meadow, where I will speedily overcome him!"

With that he strode out, mounted horse, and rode to the field. All the knights in the hall were dumb with amazement at the insult to the queen, and not one moved, so much were they astonished.

But Peredur, who was just behind the insolent knight, was stirred with anger.

"I will do vengeance upon this evil fellow!" he cried. Then he turned, and, swiftly mounting his horse, rode after the insolent knight.

But when the knight saw him coming on his bony horse, he laughed loudly. "Tell me, boy," he said, "is any knight coming to do battle with me from the court?"

"*I* will do battle with you," answered Peredur fiercely.

"I will not fight with such a scullion as you!" cried the knight in scorn. "Go back to Arthur's court, and tell the knights they are cowards, and I have shamed them all!"

"You shall fight with *me*!" said Peredur grimly. "You shall give me that goblet whose wine you dashed into the queen's face, and you shall give me your horse and armor also!"

Then in anger the knight rode at Peredur, and struck him a fierce blow in the shoulder with the butt-end of his spear.

"Would you play with me?" said Peredur. "Then I will play too."

He rode at the insolent knight and drove his sharp-pointed stick at him. It entered his eye, and immediately the knight fell from his horse and died.

Peredur leapt down, and ran to him, eager to take his armor and his horse, so that he might be dressed like a knight. But he did not know how to undo the fastenings of the armor, and he could not drag it off, try how he would.

Then Sir Owain galloping up, hot from Arthur's court, and stopped in amazement to see the arrogant knight slain by an unskilled youth, whose only weapon was a stick.

"What are you trying to do with his armor?" he asked.

"I want it for myself," said Peredur, "but I cannot undo the fastenings."

"Leave the dead knight his arms," said Sir Owain. "I will gladly give you my own horse and armor. But first come with me to Arthur and he will knight you, for you have proved yourself well worthy of the honor."

"I accept your gift," said Peredur, rising. "But I will not come to Arthur's court until I have proved myself in other adventures."

Sir Owain helped the youth to put his armor on, and then gave him his own fine horse. He bade the bold lad farewell, and watched him ride off to seek further adventures.

Peredur, rejoicing in his new arms and steed, rode on gaily. Many a knight he met on his way, and jousted with them. He overthrew each one, but spared every man's life, only bidding him go to Arthur's court and say that Peredur had sent him.

Then one night he arrived at a castle, and begged for food and shelter till the morning. He gained admittance, and a meal was set for him at the table of the lady who owned the castle. But sadness and gloom hung over the countess, and the meal was poor, for two nuns brought in six loaves and a decanter of wine, and that was all the food there was.

"Pardon the poor fare," said the countess, blushing, "but I am in great trouble."

"Tell me your distress, and I will help you," said Peredur.

"There is a wicked baron near here, who wishes to marry me," said the lady. "I refused his offer, and because of this he has taken all my lands from me, and left me only this castle. All my servants are fled, and there is no food left save the loaves and wine which some kind nuns have brought me."

"Tomorrow I will do battle with this robber!" said Peredur eagerly. "I will overthrow him, and force him to return to you all those things that he has stolen."

The next day Peredur put on his armor and rode out to meet the baron. He saw a great host spread over the plain, and riding out from it a proud knight on a beautiful black charger. He was the baron, and scornfully he accepted Peredur's challenge to fight.

Fiercely the two rode at one another, and met with such force that the baron was thrown off his horse, and lay on the ground stunned. Peredur at once dismounted and, drawing his sword, he ran to his foe. He stood over the fallen man, who, as soon as he came to his senses, saw that he was about to be slain.

"Mercy, I pray you, mercy!" he groaned.

"Mercy you shall have, but only when you earn it," said Peredur sternly. "First you must break up your army, then you must restore threefold to the countess what you have taken from her, and last of all you must submit yourself to her as her servant."

The baron groaned again, and promised to do all that Peredur demanded. The youth let him rise, and then rode back to the castle. Here he stayed until the baron had fulfilled his promises, and then proudly he rode away.

As it chanced, Arthur's camp lay near by, for the king, hearing great tales of Peredur's prowess, had come in search of him. Sir Owain saw the youth as he stood by a stream, and rode up to ask his name. As soon as he saw it was Peredur, he welcomed him gladly, and bade him go with him to Arthur.

Peredur rode to the camp, where the king smiled upon him, and bade him take his rightful place among the brave Knights of the Round Table. Then Sir Peredur, proud and glad, rode back to the court with valiant knights for company, and with an exultant heart sat down for the first time at the Round Table. Many were the brave and bold deeds he did, and he was soon famed throughout the kingdom for his courage and his daring.

The Quest of the Holy Grail

It happened one year at Pentecost that all the knights went to hear service in the chapel. When they came forth, each took his seat at the Round Table. Every place was filled save one, the Siege Perilous, in which no knight dare sit save only he that was without stain of sin.

That morning, as the knights went to take their places, they saw that something was written on the Siege Perilous in letters of gold. This is what they read: *Four hundred and fifty years after the Passion of our Lord Jesus Christ shall this seat be filled.*

Then all the knights were amazed, for when Sir Lancelot made a reckoning, it was found that exactly four hundred and fifty years had gone by – therefore the Siege Perilous should that day be filled.

As the knights stood marveling, there came a squire to the king, and told him of a wonderous sight.

"Sir," said he, "floating down the river is a stone, and in it is a sword."

"I will see this marvel," said the King.

So he and all his knights went out to the river, and there they saw the stone floating. It was of red marble, and in it was thrust a fair sword, on which were written these words: *Never shall man take me hence, but only he by whose side I ought to hang, and he shall be the best knight in the world.*

"Sir Lancelot, surely this sword belongs to you," said Arthur. "Take it, I pray you."

But Sir Lancelot, brave and noble knight though he was, knew well that he was not the best in the world, and he would not take the sword. Sir Gawaine tried, and Sir Percivale, but they could not move the sword from the great red stone. Many others tried also, but not one was strong enough to take the fair weapon from its place.

"Let us return to our meat," said Arthur. "This sword belongs to none of you."

The knights left the river, and went back to the Round Table, where each took his seat. Soon all were filled save only the Siege Perilous. Then another marvel came, and every knight sat silent in wonder.

Suddenly all the doors and windows of the hall were closed by unseen hands. Then there appeared an old man, dressed all in white, and by him walked a young knight in red armor, without sword or shield, and with an empty scabbard by his side.

"Sir King," said the old man, "I bring you here a young knight of kingly descent. Through him shall many marvels be wrought."

"You are very welcome," answered the king.

Then the old man unarmed the young knight, and took him to the Siege Perilous. He lifted up the silken cloth that covered the seat, and there, instead of the words that had been seen before, were new ones.

"This is the seat of Galahad, the high prince," shone out in letters of gold.

The young knight sat down in the seat. The old man went forth, leaving him alone in the midst of the knights. They looked at Galahad in the greatest awe and wonder, for none had ever dared to sit in the place before.

"He is so young," murmured the knights among themselves. "But he is pure of heart and without sin, and his countenance is fair and truthful."

When the company arose from the table, the king took the young knight to the river, and showed him the stone in which was the sword.

Galahad put forth his hand and drew the sword from the stone lightly and easily. He slipped it into his empty scabbard, glad to have such a fair weapon. But as yet he had no shield.

Now that evening, as the knights sat again at the Round Table, they heard the rumbling of heavy thunder so near that it seemed as if the roof were about to fall in upon them. Then, stealing into the great hall, came a sunbeam seven times brighter than any they had ever seen. In its light the knights looked upon one another, and each of them seemed fairer of face and nobler than before.

Then gliding into the sunbeam came the Holy Grail, covered with a silken cloth, so that none could see it nor who held it. Every knight was filled with happiness and awe, and gazed upon the strange sight in silence.

Suddenly it vanished. The knights drew breath again, and gave thanks to God for the good grace he had sent them.

The Holy Grail was the sacred cup out of which the Lord Jesus Christ had drunk before he died. It was sometimes seen by mortal men, but only by those who were pure of heart. The knights had not seen it completely – for it had been covered by the silken cloth.

Then Sir Gawaine sprang to his feet, and made a vow.

"I will go in search of the Holy Grail!" he cried. "I will seek for it until I see it uncovered. If I cannot find it within a year and a day, I will return, knowing that it is not for me."

All the other knights leapt up too, and made the same holy vow; but King Arthur was sad, for he knew that the quest would break up his brave company of the Round Table.

"Never again shall we all meet here," he said. "Some of you will die, some will be slain – only a few will return to me. The evil days have begun."

On the morrow the king arrayed all his knights before him, and there were a hundred and fifty. Then they bade him farewell, mounted their horses, and rode away. The people of the town were sad when they went, for they were the noblest company that ever was seen. The king wept also, for never again would he see the Round Table filled with all his noble fellowship of knights.

With the knights went Sir Galahad in his red armor, the youngest of them all. His adventures we follow, for it was he who fulfilled the quest.

The Adventures of Sir Galahad

Sir Galahad rode onwards for four days without adventure. Then he came to a White Abbey, where he found another knight of the Round Table, King Bagdemagus.

"What brings you here?" asked Galahad.

"Sir," said Bagdemagus, "there is a wonderful shield here, which must only be worn by the best knight in the world. I know well that I am not the best knight, but I shall take the shield and wear it, and see what adventure befalls me."

"He who wears the shield wrongfully shall meet death or great misfortune within three days," said a monk. "Look to yourself, King Bagdemagus, for only he to whom it belongs may wear it without harm."

"I will wear it," said the king. "If aught happens to me then Galahad shall try it next."

The next day the monk took the two knights to where the shield hung behind an altar. It was as white as snow, and in the middle was a red cross. Bagdemagus took it and slung it about his neck.

"Abide you here until you learn how I fare," he said to Galahad. Then set forth, followed by his squire.

Now he had hardly gone two miles when a knight, clad all in white armor, and seated on a white horse, came riding swiftly towards him. The king saw that he was about to fight him, and he got ready his spear. The two galloped hard upon one another, and Bagdemagus broke his spear upon the other's shield. But the White Knight smote him so hard that his spear broke the king's armor, and went right into his shoulder. He fell from his horse, and lay still on the ground. Then the White Knight dismounted, and took away the shield from the king.

"Your folly is great," he said. "This shield is not yours."

Then he took it to the squire, and gave it to him, saying: "Bear this shield to the good knight Sir Galahad, for it belongs to him."

"Sir," said the squire in awe, "what is your name?"

"That is not for you or any earthly man to know," said the White Knight.

So the squire took the shield to Galahad, who hung it about his neck with gladness. Then he went to fetch Bagdemagus, who lay ill of his wounds for many months, but escaped at last with his life.

Sir Galahad rode on his way until he came to an old chapel, where he knelt to pray; and as he prayed a voice came to him that said: "Go now, adventurous knight, to the Castle of Maidens, there to do away with its wicked customs."

The knight took horse again, and rode on till he saw before him a strong castle with deep ditches. There he saw an old man, and asked him the castle's name.

"Fair sir," said the old man, "it is the Castle of Maidens. Therein live seven wicked knights who are brothers. They lie in wait for knights and their ladies. When they have killed the knights, they take their damsels, and imprison them in the castle, so that nothing but weeping and wailing is heard there day and night."

"I will do battle with these evil knights," said Galahad. He rode on towards the castle, and suddenly out from the gates there came rushing the seven knights.

"Now you have met your death!" they cried to Galahad.

"Are you all going to fight me at once?" asked the knight.

"Yes; therefore look to yourself!" they shouted.

Galahad, undismayed, rode at the foremost knight, and smote him to earth with his spear. The second knight struck such great strokes on Galahad's shield that his spear broke. Then they drew their swords.

Galahad rode fiercely at the knights, using his sword so valiantly that he filled them with terror. They jerked their horses round, and rode away at full speed, terrified lest Galahad should pursue and kill them. But the knight let them go; he wished to enter the castle and free the imprisoned maidens.

Taking the keys from an old monk, Galahad entered and freed all those whom the wicked knights had imprisoned. With cries of gratitude and joy the maidens flocked round the young knight and thanked him.

Then Galahad summoned all the knights of the country round about, and bade them do homage to the maiden to whom the castle belonged, and promise to serve her faithfully and well. Then the next day he set out once again on his adventures.

As he departed there came a messenger to him, telling him that the seven wicked knights had met Sir Gawaine, Sir Gareth, and Sir Owain, and had been slain by them in fair battle.

"That is good news," said Galahad. "They will return no more to this castle."

The young knight rode on, meeting many adventures. In all he proved himself a true and honorable man, and so great was his might that no knight could withstand him.

One day, as he rode, he encountered Sir Lancelot and Sir Percivale. Neither of them knew him, for his armor was strange, and they challenged him to joust with them. The knight accepted the challenge, longing to prove his strength against two such famous knights as these.

He rode at Sir Lancelot, whose spear broke on Galahad's shield. So mighty was the blow Galahad gave that Lancelot was smitten to earth with his horse. Then the young knight drew his sword, and rode at Sir Percivale. He smote him on the helmet, and the sturdy knight fell straight out of his saddle.

Then, before the two knights could find out who he was, Galahad rode away, marveling that he had been able to hold his own so well with Lancelot and Percivale – for each was famous in jousts and tournaments, and much feared in battle.

There came a day when Galahad rode to the seashore. There he met a maiden, and she bade him enter a ship, saying that he should soon see the highest adventure that ever any knight saw.

When the knight stepped on board, he found Sir Percivale and Sir Bors there, and they welcomed him gladly. As the ship sailed on her way, they each told their adventures, and marveled at them.

At last they arrived at the castle of King Pelles, and he welcomed them with joy. That night the vision of the Holy Grail came to the three knights. They saw it shining under its silken covering, on a table of silver. Angels came and set candles on the table, and bade the knights come to eat the holy bread.

Tremblingly they came. Then a voice spoke to them, bidding them take the silver table and the Holy Grail to the city of Sarras, where more marvels should be done.

"Tonight the Holy Grail shall depart from this place," said the voice, "but you must go to the sea-shore three days' ride from here, and there you will find a ship, in which you will once again see the silver table and the Holy Grail. This ship shall take you to the city of Sarras."

The listening knights obeyed the commands of the holy voice. When the silver table and the Holy Grail vanished, they took horse, and rode for three days until they came to the sea-shore. There they found a ship, and when they went on board they saw in the middle of it the silver table, and on it the Holy Grail, covered with red samite.

Then Galahad fell upon his knees, and prayed for the day to come when he might see the Holy Grail uncovered, and might join his Lord Jesus Christ in Heaven.

Soon the ship came to the city of Sarras. The three knights landed, taking with them the silver table. But it was very heavy, and Galahad, seeing an old man sitting at the gate of the city, called to him to come and help.

"Truly," said the old man, " it is ten years since I was able to stand upright; I cannot help you."

"Do not think of that," said Galahad. "Rise up and come."

The old man tried to stand – and to his great amazement he found that he could do so. His crooked bones became straight, and he could walk without crutches. Then joyfully he ran to the silver table, and helped the three knights to carry it.

It was not long before the whole city knew of the miracle. The king heard the wonderful story, and commanded the knights to come before him.

They obeyed, and told him of the marvelous table of

silver, the Holy Grail, and the voice that had bade them
come to the city of Sarras.

But the king was a heathen, and when he heard of the
God of the three knights he was angry, and gave commands that they should all be thrown into prison. For a
whole year they lay there, forgotten by everyone.

Then the wicked king fell ill, and remembered the
three knights. He asked for them to be brought to him,
and when they came he begged their forgiveness, which
they gave him.

Soon afterwards he died, and the people of Sarras did
not know whom to choose for their next king. Then, as
they talked one with another, there came a voice among
them.

"You shall choose the youngest knight of the three to
be your king," said the Voice. The people listened in
awe, and made haste to obey. They took Galahad, and
crowned him, begging him to rule them, and to give
them good laws.

The young knight could not refuse, for they would
have slain him. He accepted the crown, and for a year he
ruled Sarras wisely.

At the beginning of the second year Galahad went
with Percivale and Bors to the chapel where the silver
table was kept. As soon as Galahad entered he saw an
old man there, surrounded by angels.

"Come hither," said the old man to Galahad. "Thou

shalt now see what thou hast always longed to see."

Then Galahad knew that he was about to see the Holy Grail uncovered, and that the vision would be glorious beyond compare. He began to tremble, for he was afraid of such great joy. He went to Percivale and kissed him, and then to Bors, bidding each knight farewell.

Then he went to the table and knelt down among the angels. Soon, in a dazzling light, he saw the Holy Grail uncovered, and the vision was so marvelous that the young knight prayed he might ascend to heaven at that moment. He had no wish to live longer in the world after his vision of heavenly things.

His prayer was granted, for even as he prayed his soul left his body, and was borne upwards by angels.

This was seen by Sir Percivale and Sir Bors, who saw also a hand, which came down from heaven and took away the Holy Grail.

When the angels had gone, and the chapel was once more empty, the two trembling knights saw that Galahad was still kneeling at the holy table. They went to him — but he was dead, for the angels had taken his soul, as they had seen.

Then they lamented, for they had loved him. They buried him with honor, and all the people of the city sorrowed. Then Sir Bors entered a hermitage, and became a monk; but Sir Percivale took ship, and went back to his own land. He rode to King Arthur's court, and there told

him of Sir Galahad's marvelous vision, and of how he had died in the seeing of it.

"Now the quest of the Holy Grail is ended," said King Arthur. "The best knight in the world has seen it, and no man shall dare to say hereafter that his eyes have beheld the vision."

The king spoke truly, for since then there has never been a man pure enough and strong enough to say that he has seen the Holy Grail.

Sir Mordred's Plot

There were two knights of Arthur's court, Sir Mordred and Sir Agravaine, who hated Sir Lancelot, for he was always first in tournaments, and all men spoke well of him. The king and queen loved and honored him more than any other knight.

Sir Mordred was bitterly jealous, and at last the hatred he felt grew so fierce that he longed to harm Sir Lancelot and make the king think evil of him.

So he and Sir Agravaine went about saying that Lancelot and the queen plotted treason against Arthur. Their three brothers, Sir Gawaine, Sir Gareth, and Sir Gaheris, heard these false words, and commanded Sir Mordred to cease the saying of them.

"We will tell the king himself," said Sir Mordred fiercely. At that the five brothers began to quarrel. Then the three younger ones strode away in anger, unable to make Sir Mordred and Sir Agravaine promise to hold their lying tongues.

The king heard their quarrel, and bade Sir Mordred tell him what all the noise was about.

"Sir," said Mordred, "I will keep silence no longer. Here is a thing you should know. Queen Guinevere and Sir Lancelot love one another, and because of their love they are plotting treason against you."

Arthur loved Sir Lancelot with all his heart, and he would not believe what Sir Mordred said. The wicked knight left him in rage, vowing that he would prove to the king that what he said was true.

He waited until Arthur had gone on a journey, and had left Guinevere behind. As was her custom, she sent for Lancelot to come and talk with her in the evening. He went to her, clad in a rich mantle, and unarmed. He did not dream that Sir Mordred and Sir Agravaine, with twelve other knights, were hiding near by, watching.

No sooner was Lancelot in the queen's room, talking with her, than the fourteen knights leapt out from their hiding-place, and ran to the door.

"Traitor knight!" they cried, hammering on the door, "we know that you are plotting treason against the king! Open, and let us take you!"

The queen and Lancelot leapt up in surprise. The knight laid his hand to where his sword should be, and groaned when he remembered that he was unarmed. What could he do against fourteen fully armed men?

The knights outside were still shouting and hammering on the door. Then they fetched a bench, and tried to break it down. Lancelot could no longer bear the cries of "traitor" hurled at him, and he resolved to meet the knights, even if it meant his death.

He wrapped his mantle thickly round his arm, and
opened the door a little way, so that but one knight could
come in. This was a huge man, Sir Colgrevance, who
with his sword struck at Sir Lancelot mightily. But the

knight put aside the stroke and gave Sir Colgrevance such a buffet on the helmet that he fell dead to the floor.

At once Lancelot dragged the knight inside the room, shut the door again, and bolted. it. Then he stripped Sir Colgrevance of his armor and donned it himself.

He flung open the door, and stood there to face the thirteen knights. At one blow he slew Sir Agravaine, and then he stepped fiercely towards the other knights. So full of wrath was he and so mighty that not one man could withstand him. One after another he slew, and at last none was left save only the wicked Sir Mordred. Him Sir Lancelot wounded sorely, so that he fled away with all his might.

Then Lancelot returned to Guinevere and begged her to ride away with him.

"If Mordred goes with his lying tongue to the king, and tells him that there was treason between you and me against Arthur, and that I have killed Sir Agravaine and twelve other knights of the Round Table, there will be heavy punishment for us both," said Lancelot. "Come with me, where you may be safe, for Arthur in his anger may condemn you to death."

But Guinevere would not go.

"I must stay here and meet the king myself," she said.

Meanwhile Mordred was riding swiftly to Arthur, to tell him of the night's happenings. The king was amazed to see him stagger from his horse, and come to kneel before him, wounded and bleeding.

"Sir, we have proved treason," said Sir Mordred. "Also Sir Lancelot has killed Sir Agravaine and twelve other knights of your fellowship. We demand that you condemn your false queen to death."

Alas! Arthur could do nothing else, for he must keep the law of the land, which said that treason was to be punished by death. He sent for Sir Gawaine, and sadly commanded him to bring out the queen to be burnt.

"That I will never do," said Gawaine. "She is a noble lady, and you do wrong to consent to her death."

Then Arthur sent for Gawaine's younger brothers, Sir Gareth and Sir Gaheris, and bade them bring the queen to the burning. They were young and dared not disobey, but their hearts were very heavy.

"We will obey," said Gareth. "But it is a hard thing you have commanded us."

When the day came, the queen was fetched to the burning, and many lords and ladies wept to see her, so pale she was and sorrowful. Only Mordred and his company were merry, for they knew that the queen's death would mean terrible sorrow to Lancelot, the knight they so bitterly hated.

But that brave knight was not going to let Guinevere suffer death for his sake. He waited until she had been tied to the stake, and then he galloped up, scattering aside all those who were in his way. Mordred and his friends drew their swords and attacked him; but never was there a knight who could withstand Lancelot. He laid about him with vigor and his enemies were down before him, wounded or dead.

He hacked his way to the stake, and then cut Guinevere's bonds with his sword. He swung her up on his horse, and, sword in hand, galloped away again, none daring to stop him, so terrible was his might. But little did Lancelot know what he had done in his slaying – for he had all unawares killed both Sir Gareth and Sir Gaheris, brothers of Sir Gawaine. In the heat and the press he had not seen them, and his avenging sword had slain them among his enemies. They lay dead beside the stake.

When it was told to Arthur that the two young knights had been slain by Lancelot, he sat in great anguish of heart, for he knew that Sir Gawaine, their brother, would be overcome with grief.

When Gawaine came in, he asked for news, and it was

told him that Lancelot had rescued the queen from her burning.

"That was knightly done," said Gawaine. "But where are my two brothers?"

"They are slain," answered the man who had brought the news.

"That cannot be," said Gawaine. "Who should slay them?"

"Sir Lancelot slew them," said the messenger. "They lie dead beside the stake."

Then Gawaine gave a dreadful cry and ran to Arthur.

"My lord, my lord," he said, with the tears bursting from his eyes, "my two brothers are slain on Lancelot's sword."

"Take comfort, Gawaine," said the king, himself weeping with sorrow. "Lancelot killed them in the great press around him, and did not know that they were there."

"O my two fair brothers!" said Gawaine, almost out of his senses with grief. "Never will I rest until I have avenged their deaths. Henceforth all my life I will spend in striving to slay the evil knight who slew my brothers!"

Then King Arthur looked with unhappy eyes into the future – for he knew that his noble fellowship of the Round Table was for ever broken.

Sir Gawaine meets Sir Lancelot

Sir Gawaine would not let King Arthur rest, but bade him take arms against Sir Lancelot, and do battle with him. So the king marched against the knight's castle, and grievous was the killing on the battlefield, and many a noble knight was slain.

Then the Pope of Rome heard that the two greatest knights of the world, King Arthur and Sir Lancelot, were at war one with another. He sent a message to each, bidding them cease.

He commanded Lancelot to return Guinevere to the king, and he bade Arthur take her back in peace and forgiveness. Each promised to obey, and when the day came for Lancelot to ride to the court with Guinevere, there was great stir among the knights and lords on both sides.

The king sat waiting in his great hall, with his knights about him. Then came Sir Lancelot riding with the queen, and they entered the hall, and knelt before Arthur.

"I bring you your queen," said Lancelot to the king, "and, my lord, there is no truer or more honorable lady in the land, and I will do battle with any knight who denies my words."

But none spoke, not even Gawaine, for though he hated Lancelot bitterly, he had always honored the queen.

The king looked sadly on Sir Lancelot, for he had loved him well.

"You were my best-loved knight," he said. "And now you have brought great sorrow upon me."

"If you speak of the slaying of Sir Gareth and of Sir Gaheris," said Sir Lancelot," there is no man alive feels more sorrow for that than myself, for I held both knights in love and honor, and Sir Gareth was knighted by me."

"You are a traitor," said Sir Gawaine fiercely, "and never will I forgive you for slaying my two fair brothers. If my lord Arthur will not fight for me, and avenge their deaths, then I will leave him, and I and my friends will do battle with you alone."

"Peace, Gawaine!" said Arthur. "Sir Lancelot, you must leave the kingdom, and see that before fifteen days are past, you and all your men are gone."

Then Lancelot looked around the hall, and was heavy of heart, for he knew that never again would he sit at the Round Table with his friends. And many there were who wept to see that noble knight depart, but none spoke him farewell.

Very soon Lancelot gathered all his kinsmen together, and departed to France, where he had great lands. But even when he was gone Gawaine could not forget the vow he had made to avenge his brothers' deaths by slaying Lancelot.

"My lord king," he said to Arthur, "I pray you take your army to France, and do battle with the traitor there. Have you forgotten already how Lancelot killed Sir Gareth and Sir Gaheris, both of whom loved him so well?"

Arthur knew that if he did not consent to Gawaine's wish, the knight would leave him, and take with him his friends and kinsmen. So few of the knights were now left that the King could not bear to lose more; therefore he agreed to take an army to France, and force Lancelot to fight, though it was sorely against his will.

"I will make Sir Mordred, my nephew, ruler of my kingdom while I am gone," said King Arthur. So this was done, and the false knight rejoiced in his great power. Then over the sea went Arthur and all his host.

Sir Lancelot retired into his strong castle, and let Arthur's knights waste his lands as they would, for he could not bring himself to fight against the king he loved so well. But his own knights were angry, and begged him to let them go and fight.

"I will send to make peace," said Lancelot. "I will tell the king of the love I bear him, and maybe he will listen. If he does not, then we will fight."

So Lancelot sent a fair damsel to Arthur, charging her

to plead with the king, and to tell him that for love of him he would not fight. The damsel mounted her palfrey and rode to Arthur's camp.

Many knights there hoped that the king would listen to her pleadings, and declare peace, for there was not one that did not love and honor Lancelot as the noblest knight living. When she began to remind the king of the glorious days of the Round Table, of the friendship that had been between him and Lancelot, and of the many times that that great knight had save the king from death, Arthur wept for sorrow.

Then would he fain have told the damsel that there could be no more war between him and Lancelot, but only love and honor. But Sir Gawaine would not let the king have peace, and he turned on Arthur in anger.

"You must have your way, Sir Gawaine," said Arthur sadly. "I do not forget that this quarrel is yours, because of your fair brothers, Sir Gareth and Sir Gaheris. I will send no message to Lancelot; you shall tell the damsel what you will."

"Then return to Sir Lancelot," said Gawaine to the weeping maiden, "and tell him that so long as I have life in my body I will seek to slay him. Tell him he is a traitor and a coward, and no true knight."

The damsel departed, and rode back to the castle. When the knights there heard Gawaine's message, they were very angry, and shouted for battle. But Sir

Lancelot stood silent with the tears running down his cheeks, grieved to the heart to think that the goodly fellowship of the Round Table should be so broken up and divided against itself.

The next day the King's knights came riding round the castle. Sir Gawaine was with them, and he rode up to the walls and shouted for Lancelot.

"Where is that traitor knight?" he cried. "Where is he who plotted treason against my lord Arthur? O Lancelot, do you hide within your castle like a coward?"

Then Sir Lancelot knew that he must fight with Gawaine, or lose his honor among knights. He mounted upon his horse, and rode proudly out of the castle with all his men.

Gawaine rode to meet him, and when the armies saw these two powerful knights set against one another, they drew apart. It was arranged that no man should go near them; they should fight their battle to the end.

Sir Gawaine and Sir Lancelot galloped their horses furiously at one another, and each knight smote the other in the middle of his shield. So strong were they, and so big their spears, that the horses could not stand the shock, and both fell to earth. The knights leapt lightly off, put their shields before them, and drew their swords.

For three hours the two knights fought a hard battle, and sore were the strokes that each gave. Soon both were wounded, and the watching hosts marveled that men so sorely hurt could fight. Sir Gawaine, fierce in his great anger, was stronger than Sir Lancelot, and many a time that great knight feared to be defeated and shamed by him.

But at the end of three hours he felt Gawaine's strength go, and knew that he would vanquish him. He doubled his strokes, and gave Gawaine such a buffet on the helmet that the knight fell to the ground and could not rise again. There was no man living that could withstand the buffets of Sir Lancelot.

The knight withdrew from Gawaine, but Gawaine cried out to him: "Why do you go from me? Now turn again, false traitor knight, and slay me, for if you leave me thus, I will do battle with you again when I am whole."

"You know well, Sir Gawaine, that I would never

smite a fallen knight," said Sir Lancelot.

Then he went to his castle; and Sir Gawaine was borne to his tent, where his grievous wounds were dressed. For many weeks he lay ill, but vowed still that he would slay Sir Lancelot – for never could Gawaine forget the death of his two brothers, Sir Gareth and Sir Gaheris.

The Passing of Arthur

Now as soon as the king was gone over the sea, the false Sir Mordred gave out that Arthur had been killed in battle. He made himself king, and sent to Queen Guinevere to say that he would wed her, and she should be his queen.

The people believed that Arthur was dead, and welcomed Sir Mordred, promising to fight for him. But when it came to Arthur's ears that his nephew had usurped his throne, and meant to marry Guinevere, he was very wroth, and made haste to return to his kingdom.

Sir Mordred resolved not to let the king land, for he knew that if the people saw Arthur, they would know that their rightful king was not dead, and would go to fight under his standard. So he got ready a fleet of ships, and gave Arthur battle off the coast of Dover.

But the king's knights were very powerful, and Mordred could not prevent them from landing. There was a fierce battle, in which many knights were wounded, and then Mordred and his men fled away.

After the battle, King Arthur gave commands that those that were dead should be buried. Then was noble Sir Gawaine found in a great boat, dying. When Arthur heard this, he went to him, and took him into his arms, sorrowing his heart out.

"Sir Gawaine, my sister's son, here you lie, the man I love most. You and Sir Lancelot were my greatest friends, and now have I lost you both."

"Mine uncle, King Arthur," said Gawaine, "my death-day is come, for I am smitten upon the old wound that Sir Lancelot gave me. And now I see that by my haste and wilfulness I have brought sorrow and death to full many a knight, because I would not make peace with Lancelot. If he had been with you now, your enemies would not have dared to rise against you, for the name of Lancelot is feared and honored throughout the kingdom. Alas that I should have quarreled with such a noble knight! I pray you, mine uncle, set pen and paper before me, for I would write to Lancelot before I die."

Then, when pen and paper were set before him, Gawaine wrote his last letter:

"I, Gawaine, send you greeting, and would have you know that I am smitten upon the old wound you gave me, wherefore I am brought to my death-day. I beseech you, Sir Lancelot, return again to this kingdom and say a prayer for me at my tomb. Also, by all the love there was between us, do not tarry, but come over the sea in all haste, that you may with your noble knights rescue our well-loved lord, King Arthur, who is greatly pressed by his false nephew, Sir Mordred."

Then Sir Gawaine died, and the noble knight was buried with much honor and sorrow, for he had been greatly loved.

Sir Mordred fled to the west, and King Arthur pursued after him, resolved to give him battle and defeat him sorely. At last he came up with him, and planned with his knights to attack his enemy on the next day.

But that night Sir Gawaine came to Arthur in a dream, and warned him that if he fought on the morrow he would meet his death, and so would all his noble knights.

"Make a treaty with Sir Mordred," said Gawaine. "If you have truce for a month, then Sir Lancelot will come to you again with all his men, and you shall win a great victory. And you and Sir Lancelot shall hold one another in friendship again as heretofore."

Then Gawaine vanished, and the king awoke. He called his men around him, and told them his dream.

Then all of them declared that they must make treaty with Mordred, and delay the battle for a month.

So the next day a message was sent to Sir Mordred, asking for a council to be held, to make a treaty; and it was decided that each side should take fourteen knights to the meeting.

Before Arthur went to the council he called his chief knights before him.

"I in no way trust this false traitor, Sir Mordred," he said. "He may mean treachery, though we meet in peace. If you see the flash of a sword, see you come on fiercely, for you will know you are needed."

Then Arthur and Mordred, and fourteen knights with each, went to the council; and they agreed to make peace for a month. But as they sat at the meeting, an adder crept out of the bushes, and bit a knight on the foot.

He felt the sharp pain, and when he saw that an adder had bitten him, he drew his sword to kill it.

His weapon flashed in the sun, and both sides saw it! At once all thought that there was treachery afoot, for the watching hosts

could not see the adder. Then trumpets and horns blew loudly, men shouted, and the two armies ranged themselves to fight.

"Alas, this unhappy day!" said King Arthur. He mounted his horse, and rode back to his host, while Sir Mordred did likewise.

Then began a fearful battle, and great blows were given on either side. Brave knights fell by the hundred, and many daring deeds were done. All day long the battle raged, and of all the knights there was none so brave as King Arthur himself.

When evening drew on, the king looked around him. He groaned in dismay and sorrow when he beheld, of all his noble company of knights, but two alive, and they were sorely wounded. Sir Lucan and Sir Bedivere were the knights, and they went to their lord in sorrow.

On the other side there was one knight left, and he was Sir Mordred. The battlefield was strewn with hundreds of dead, and it was a sight to make the bravest man weep.

"Alas, that ever I should see this doleful day!" said the king. "Where are all my noble knights? Would to God I knew where that traitor Sir Mordred is, that has caused all this mischief."

As he spoke, he saw Mordred not very far distant, leaning on his sword among a great heap of dead men.

"Now give me my spear," said Arthur to Sir Lucan. "I

will slay this traitor with mine own hand."

Then, with his great spear in his hand, the king ran towards Sir Mordred, crying, "Traitor! Now is thy death-day come!"

He thrust with great might through sir Mordred's shield, and the spear entered the traitor's body, standing out behind a good way. Mordred knew that he had received his death-stroke, and with his last remaining strength, he took hold of his sword with both hands, and brought it down upon King Arthur's helmet. Then he fell back and died.

Arthur sank to earth in a swoon, for his head had been cleft by the sword. Sir Lucan and Sir Bedivere came to him, and lifted him up to carry him to a place of shelter. But Sir Lucan's wound was so great that his brave heart burst, and he fell dead by Arthur's side.

When Arthur came to his senses, and saw Sir Lucan there, and his brother Sir Bedivere weeping by him, he could scarcely speak for sorrow.

"Sir Bedivere," he said at last, "I would have you do a thing for me. Take Excalibur, my good sword, and go with it to yonder waterside. Throw it into the water, and then return to me again to tell me what you see."

Sir Bedivere took the sword and departed. But on the way to the water he looked at the beautiful weapon, and grieved to think that it should be thrown away.

So he hid Excalibur under a tree, and returned to the

king, saying that he had done as he was commanded.

"What did you see when you threw the sword into the water?" asked the king.

"Nothing but waves and wind," said the knight.

"You speak falsely," said Arthur sadly. "Go again to the water, and throw the sword in, as I bade you."

Then Sir Bedivere turned again, and fetched the sword, to do the king's bidding. But again he looked at the noble weapon, and thought it great shame to fling it away. So once more he hid it beneath a tree, and returned to Arthur.

"What did you see this time?" asked the king.

"Nothing but the rippling of the water," answered the knight.

"Ah, traitor untrue!" said the king. "Now you have betrayed me twice. Do as I command you, or with my own hands I will slay you, for you are no true knight to me, Sir Bedivere, if you will not do my last wish."

Then Sir Bedivere was ashamed, and taking the sword he went with it to the water. He threw it out as far as he might. Then there came an arm above the water, and caught the sword, brandished it three times, and so vanished.

Then the knight returned to the king, and told him what he had seen, and Arthur was content. Sir Bedivere took him upon his back, and carried him to the water-side; and there came by a barge with many fair ladies in it, with black hoods, crying and wailing.

"Now put me into the barge," said King Arthur, and it was done. Then the barge was rowed out from the land, leaving Sir Bedivere alone by the waterside.

"Ah, my lord Arthur," cried the dismayed knight," what shall become of me, now that you are gone, and I am alone?"

"Comfort yourself," said the king. "I go to the Island of Avalon, to heal me of my grievous wound, and if you hear of me nevermore, pray for my soul."

Then the barge passed out of sight. Sir Bedivere gave a dolorous cry, and fled into the forest weeping and wailing.

No more is written of the great King Arthur, but there are some that say he is not dead, but dwells still in the happy Island of Avalon, from whence he will come again when his kingdom needs him.

Others say that he is indeed dead, and that his tomb lies in the distant West. On it is written these words:

"Here lies Arthur,
once King
and King to be."